To Lillie

Jasper Tomkins
1993

THE MOUNTAINS CRACK UP!

Written and illustrated by Jasper Tomkins

GREEN TIGER PRESS
Published by Simon & Schuster
New York London Toronto Sydney Tokyo Singapore

For a mountain of a grandfather

GREEN TIGER PRESS
Simon & Schuster Building, Rockefeller Center
1230 Avenue of the Americas, New York, New York 10020
Copyright © 1987 by Jasper Tomkins
All rights reserved including the right of reproduction
in whole or in part in any form.
GREEN TIGER PRESS is an imprint of Simon & Schuster.
Manufactured in Singapore

10   9   8   7   6   5

ISBN: 0-671-75273-1

The typeface is Artcraft Light, set by Professional Typography
of San Diego, California

Once there were three mountains ...

who ordered their favorite animals from a catalog. Of course, the animals had to eat, so they ordered refrigerators full of food. And just for fun, the mountains ordered flashlights for the giraffes, decks of cards for the turtles, and a record player for the bears.

The nights were getting colder and colder, and the animals needed a warm place to sleep. Finally, one little bear secretly ordered three big hats for the mountains. And from then on they all slept safe and cozy every night.

One cold morning the animals woke up to find little white things falling from the sky. "Maybe they are messages," said a giraffe. "Maybe they are dangerous," said a turtle. "No, I think they are pieces of white bread," said a hungry bear as he caught one with his paw.

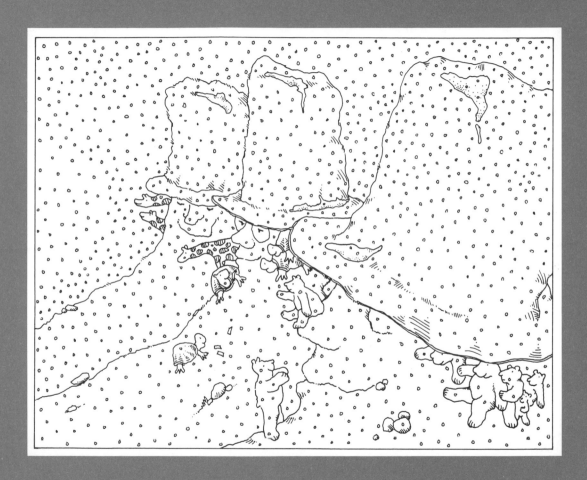

When the ground was completely white, three bears took a test walk. They liked the sound of their crunchy footsteps and the feeling of the snow between their toes. After a short distance they turned around and laughed when they saw their big footprints. Then they yelled for the others to come and join the fun.

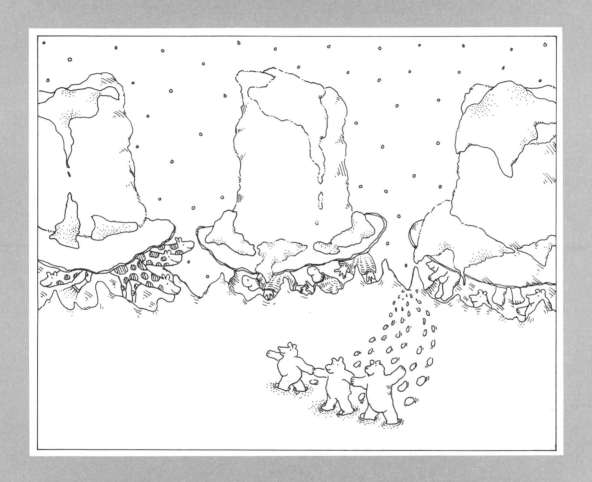

What a wonderful winter it was!
The giraffes liked to pretend that they
were sharks. The turtles played on their
built-in sleds. And the bears fell over
backwards and made bear angels.
    The mountains were thrilled to see all
this activity. The hats kept the snow off
their eyes.

When the wild blizzards came, the animals crawled under the turtles' hat because it felt safe to be in the middle. Of course, they all played cards until the storm was over.

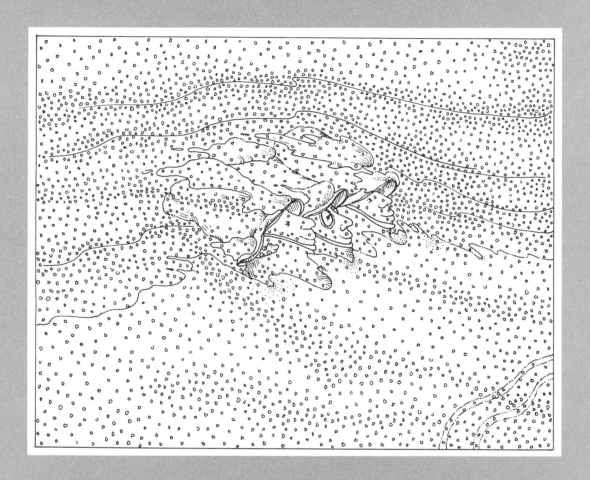

As winter passed and the sun rose higher and higher, the snow began to melt. It dripped and dripped until finally one grand spring day it was time to take off the hats.

It was quite a day of work.

When the hats were safely back in their boxes, the animals all took a nap in the warm sun. The mountains felt the wind again, and listened to the birds.

One little bear who was very hungry quietly tip-toed to the refrigerator for a snack. While he was eating he noticed that the three mailboxes were just reappearing from under the melting snow. He ran down to see if there might be any mail.

To his surprise there was only one envelope from the whole winter. The little bear opened it up and cried out with astonishment. It was the bill for everything they had ordered from the catalog. He ran back to tell the others.

That night they had a big meeting. Everyone was concerned. There were many ideas about how to pay the bill. Finally one mountain suggested that they ask the grandfather mountains for advice. They all agreed it was the best thing to do.

The next morning, five of the bears had an early breakfast. When their tummies were full they went down to the mailboxes to wait for the mail truck.

When the truck pulled to a stop, the driver told the bears that they had to sit in the back, hold their stamps, and be quiet like the rest of the packages. It was a long bumpy journey, but finally, just before sunset, they stopped at the grandfather mountains' mailboxes.

The bears walked up the path,
and then they stopped and stared in
amazement. There were the grandfather
mountains!
   The bears did not know what to say.
"Good evening," boomed the mountains.
"Hello," said the bears, and then they
began to tell the story of the bill.

When the bears were finished, the mountains began to laugh. "You are all such treasures! How can you be in debt?" The bears were puzzled but could not help laughing.

Then the grandfather mountains smiled at the bears. "It is important that you rest. We will be thinking while you sleep." The bears were quite relieved and curled up in a cozy cave.

In the middle of the night they heard the mountains whispering about hats. The bears smiled and went back to sleep.

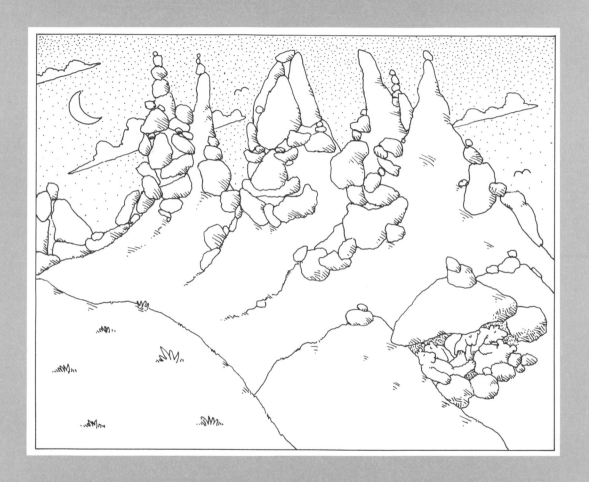

In the morning the mountains had a curious answer for the bears. All that they would say was, "Go now and be happy. Your laughter will pay the bill."

That was all. The puzzled bears ran down to the mailbox just in time. And as they piled into the mail truck they could still hear the laughter echoing in the distance.

As soon as the bears were home they gathered everyone together and told the story of their journey. But when they finished there were no smiles. There was no laughter. The mountains and the animals just did not see how being happy would pay the bill.

The five bears knew that this would never do! They would have to do something quickly. Suddenly one little bear ran up and whispered something to one of the mountains. The mountain smiled. Then it chuckled. Then it began to laugh; harder and harder.

Soon all three mountains were laughing. They began to shake with laughter. It was an earthquake of laughter. The rocks were rolling down, and the animals were bouncing every which way. But they were laughing so hard themselves that they were not even frightened.

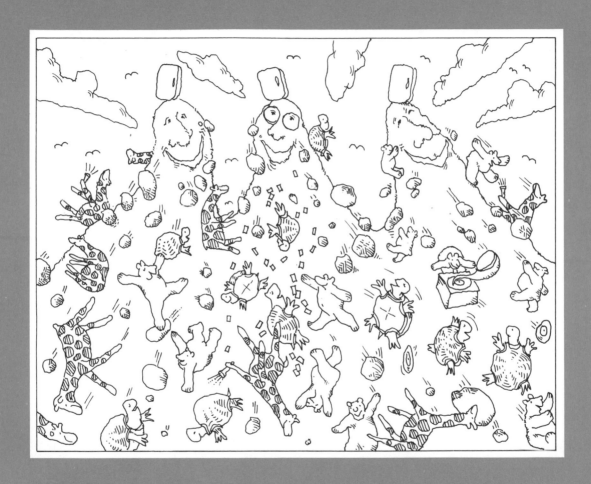

It seemed that the wonderful laughter would never end. But finally everyone simply had to stop and catch his breath. In the quiet moment that followed one little bear said he felt like he was glowing. "So do we," exclaimed the mountains. And they were!

"You *are* glowing!" shouted the animals, and they all stared in amazement. The shaking laughter had uncovered bright, shining crystals all over the mountains. They were flashing in the sunset light. The animals ran to pick them up.

Now the five bears knew just what the grandfather mountains had meant. They ran to find a box. And what a time the animals had filling it up. When they were finished they stared into the box with fascination. "It is a box of light," exclaimed one giraffe.

The next morning the special box was sent to the catalog company. Of course, everyone wanted to know what the little bear had said that was so funny. But he would only giggle. And the mountains just smiled and said they felt much lighter than ever before.

Several days later a letter came from the catalog. The company was thrilled with what they found in the box. The bill had been much more than paid off. In fact there was now a large credit available. They all cheered.

The five bears immediately sent a mysterious rush order back to the catalog.

What wonderful days these had been! That night the animals all lay out under the stars and saw themselves in the universe. When sleep finally came they all had dreams of what they would order next from the catalog.

And later, while they slept, there was a rumble of laughter in the distance.

For at that very moment, the grandfather mountains were putting on their brand new hats!